THE BOUNTY HUNTER

AN OREGON TRAIL ADVENTURE

THE OREGON

LEGEND

Important forts, cities, towns, and landmarks are shown as they were in 1848. State boundaries are shown as they are today.

- ● ● ● ● Oregon Trail
- ★ Forts
- ▫ Cities, towns
- ▽ Landmarks

TRAIL

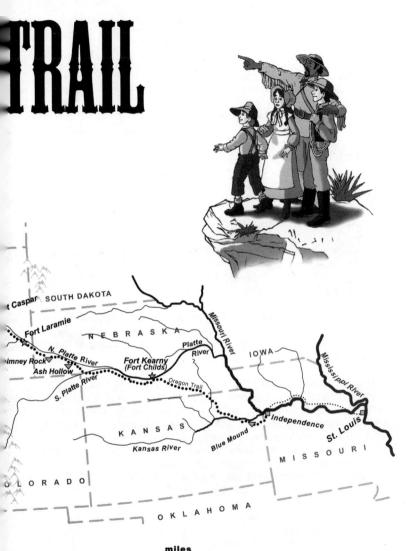

t Caspar · SOUTH DAKOTA

Fort Laramie

NEBRASKA

N. Platte River

imney Rock ▽

Ash Hollow

S. Platte River

Fort Kearny
(Fort Childs)

Platte River

Oregon Trail

IOWA

Missouri River

Mississippi River

KANSAS

Kansas River

Blue Mound

Independence

St. Louis

MISSOURI

OLORADO

OKLAHOMA

miles

0   100   200

0   150   300

kilometers

Other titles in this series:
Westward Bound!
Ride to Rescue

Learning Company Books
A Division of Riverdeep, Inc.
500 Redwood Boulevard, Novato, CA 94947, USA

Editor: Brenda Kienan
Cover Illustration: David Hicock
Illustrations: Animotion, Inc.
Page layout: Black Dot Group

ISBN 0-7630-7725-9

First printing: May 2004
Printed in the United States of America

10 9 8 7 6 5 4 3 2 1

**Visit Learning Company Books at
www.learningcompanybooks.com.**

THE BOUNTY HUNTER

AN OREGON TRAIL ADVENTURE

Mel Friedman

Learning Company Books
A division of Riverdeep, Inc.

BY THE RISING CAW

Steam was rising from the backs of sweating oxen and mules as the wagon train approached the banks of the Kansas River just after dawn. The people on the wagon train showed signs of fatigue too. With their wagons packed with food and possessions, there was little room for anyone to ride inside. So the Oregon-bound pioneers were walking down the trail, just like their draft animals. The men and boys driving the oxen and mule teams marched beside the animals, directing their movements with swift cries and the loud cracking of whips over the animals' heads.

Captain Jed Freedman, the traveling party's guide, signaled to the drivers to circle their wagons in a large meadow by the water. After the last of the ten wagons had creaked to a halt, the pioneers unhitched their draft animals and let them graze freely inside the makeshift corral.

Soon the rest stop was buzzing with activity as some pioneers began preparing their wagons for the first big test of their river-crossing skills since they'd left Independence, Missouri, their jumping-off point, about a week ago.

"Throw down some blocks!" fifteen-year-old Parker Montgomery called up to his younger brother Jimmy. Jimmy was standing barefoot on a long wooden plank secured above the jockey box, a tool box attached to the front of the family's small covered farm wagon.

Jimmy wasn't paying attention. He wasn't doing so out of laziness or orneriness, though. He had just drifted off (as he often did) into his own private dream world. By chance the Montgomery wagon had parked on the crest of a gently sloping hill that offered a breathtaking view of the winding river and the lush grasslands beyond. It was a sight that was guaranteed to hold Jimmy spellbound. A budding artist whose gift for lifelike drawing was strikingly apparent, even at age ten, he eagerly drank in the scenery, as if trying to memorize every detail for his next charcoal sketch.

"Hey, Parker!" Jimmy cried. "C'mon up here. You can see for miles."

"Blocks first," Parker repeated.

"It's prettier than a picture!" Jimmy said.

"Don't forget what Captain Jed said," Parker admonished. "He said he's seen a lot of greenhorns wreck their wagons just because they forgot to block their wheels. You don't want us rolling back downhill, do you?"

Jimmy's freckled face flushed the color of his reddish hair. He shook his head vigorously, nearly losing his floppy yellow felt hat in the gusting wind. "That'd be awful," he said. Turning, he darted through the oval opening in the wagon's curved canvas top. This tough white covering, known as a bonnet, protected the pioneers and their belongings from choking trail dust, driving rain, and harsh weather. Moments later, Jimmy emerged, smiling, carrying two square wooden blocks, which he carefully lowered down to his brother.

"Thanks, Jimmy," Parker said. "Now how about tacklin' another chore before Captain Jed comes by on his rounds?"

"You want me to shoot a buffalo? I can, you know. I've been practicing with a stick."

"Not exactly," replied Parker. "Cassie's down by the river fetching water. I bet sis could use a strong fella to help with the buckets. Then we'll all take a short break and climb up and look at your view."

"Promise?" said Jimmy.

"Cross my heart."

"It's a deal," Jimmy said.

Parker grinned as Jimmy sprang off the wagon and dashed down the hill, making "Pow! Pow! Pow!" shooting noises as he ran. Parker was pleased to see Jimmy acting happy again. There hadn't been much to smile about in the Montgomery family for a long while—at least not since their ma died about a year ago.

Coping with the tragedy would have been much easier had their pa been around to see them through it. But he'd been clear across the continent. Smitten by "Oregon fever"—wondrous reports of an unspoiled paradise on the far side of the Cascade Mountains—their pa had left the family home in St. Louis and set out for the Oregon country in 1843. He'd always planned to send for the rest of the family as soon as he'd gotten settled and built a homestead. But by the time the call had come to get ready, it was 1848, and their ma was gone.

Pa Montgomery had originally intended to come back east to fetch the children himself, but he'd broken his leg in an accident and couldn't travel. So he did the next best thing. He'd sent his good friend Captain Jed, one of the best trail guides in the West, to escort the kids to their new home. In April of 1848, the three Montgomery children embarked on a great adventure—a perilous two thousand-mile journey across raging rivers, high mountains, and burning deserts to a new life in Oregon country.

Resuming his chores, Parker wedged the wooden stop blocks securely behind the iron tires of the two rear wheels. After checking all four wheels for wear and tear, he greased the axles and tightened the bolts on the wagon's gearing. Then he unyoked the double team of oxen and the family milk cow, St. Louis. He led the animals toward the center of the wagon circle, where he left them to munch contentedly in the field of sweet bluestem prairie grass.

When Parker returned, Cassie and Jimmy were perched on the plank above the jockey box, motioning him to join them. Parker noticed two brimming water buckets stationed on the ground next to the tongue—the long hickory pole that ran between the oxen to hitch their yokes to the wagon. He also noticed that Cassie had hung up last night's blankets and quilts to air on a rope she'd strung between the wagon and a stick she'd wedged between two rocks.

Parker planted one foot firmly on the left-front wheel hub and pulled himself up and onto the plank. Cassie, suddenly finding herself sandwiched between her two brothers, stepped back slightly to make room.

"That was a real smart idea, sis," Parker said, pointing to the clothesline.

"Thanks," Cassie said. "I just couldn't abide sleeping under those damp covers for one more night." She brushed aside a lock of brown hair that had strayed from underneath her white sunbonnet. "Maybe we can't always keep clean on this horrid trail, but we can at least try to stay dry."

Parker gazed at his thirteen-year-old sister. In many ways, she reminded him of their ma. Cassie had their ma's wide blue eyes, her slim build, and her lustrous brown hair. She had also inherited their ma's love of books, art, and music as well as her strong-willed temperament. Cassie had never been outdoorsy, preferring town life to country life and the comforts of home to the attractions of nature. As a result, Parker had worried about how well she might adapt to the demands of six months on the trail. But so far, despite her frequent complaints about all the hardships and sacrifices, Cassie seemed to be faring surprisingly well, developing her own personal brand of the pioneering spirit.

An insistent tug on Parker's shirtsleeve roused him from musings. It was Jimmy. "Didn't I tell you the view was pretty?" he said.

Parker let his eyes sweep the prairie. "You called it right, Jimmy," he said.

In the slanting morning sunlight, the Kansas River looked like a giant snake slithering through the landscape, its thick gray back glinting like a sparkler. A few wind-bent trees clutched desperately at the river banks, mostly a scattering of willows, cottonwoods, and fragrant wild plums. On the twisted limb of an old sycamore, two vultures sat, hunch-shouldered, sniffing the air, waiting to catch the scent of their next tasty meal. Beyond the river and extending as far as the eye could see was a vast sea of knee-high grass, spring green in color, that swayed to and fro at the wind's pleasure under a cloudless turquoise sky.

"Which way leads to Pa?" Cassie asked.

"Gotta be that way," Jimmy said, swinging his arm toward the left.

In the distance, on the opposite side of the river, the Montgomerys could see a trail of dust being kicked up by a line of covered wagons rolling toward the horizon. Its party of emigrants had completed the crossing the previous day and decided to pitch camp on the far shore that night. Now the caravan was once more under way— pushing, straining, and driving deeper into the Great Plains.

"That'll be us tomorrow," Parker said.

"But how're we gonna get across the water?" asked Jimmy.

"Good question, son," a voice boomed from behind. "That's what I'm fixin' to discuss with you."

Captain Jed Freedman came around the side of the wagon and placed a mud-stained boot on top of the wagon tongue. He was an imposing man, about forty-five years old, with penetrating eyes, deep brown skin, curly black hair, and a dark moustache and beard that wreathed his mouth.

The three Montgomerys plunked themselves down on the wooden board and let their legs dangle over the edge.

"Is there a problem?" Cassie inquired innocently. "I was just down by the river. It doesn't look too deep. Can't our oxen pull us across?"

Captain Jed shook his head. "The Caw's running higher than our wagon bottoms," he said, using the Indian name for the Kansas River. "If you try to drive your wagon into the current, your oxen will be swimmin' for dear life—and your wagon will be swamped in no time."

Cassie looked aghast. "Then we won't cross here. Let's find a better spot."

Captain Jed shook his head again. "I know the Caw as good as anyone. There's no better spot in fifty miles."

"But I've got Ma's trunk and Grandma's quilt and my books and the trail journal Grandpa Montgomery made for me and my one fancy dress and—"

"Just calm down, sis," interrupted Parker. He turned to Captain Jed. "So if we can't ford the Caw, what are our choices?"

"Only two, actually," the veteran guide replied. "Upriver a bit there's a ferry. It'll take you and the animals across the Caw for a fee. Some of our wagon train members have decided to take it. You could too."

"Is it safe?" Cassie asked.

"Mostly," Captain Jed said. "But I won't lie to you. This ferry's smaller than the scow that took us across the Missouri from Independence. And I've seen a few ferries sink in bad weather or tip if a load shifts."

"How's the fare?" asked Parker, who was always concerned with money matters.

"Not fair enough, if you ask me. Four dollars for the wagon plus twenty-five cents for each draft animal plus ten cents for every one of us."

Parker whistled softly. "That comes to five dollars and sixty-five cents."

"Let's do it," urged Cassie. "We've got some cash saved up. I don't want to risk ruining our things!"

"Not so fast, Cassie!" Parker said. "Five-sixty-five is a lot of money. We've already spent a fortune on the steamboat from St. Louis and the Missouri scow. It's crazy to squander our savings now. We've got a long way to go on this trail. What if the wagon bonnet tears or the oxen die and we've got no money left? What'll we do then?"

"If it happens out in the wilderness, it won't matter," Cassie snapped back. "What good is money in the middle of nowhere? Better to spend it wisely while we can."

There was a loud clanging noise. Jimmy had grabbed a cowbell from the wagon and was ringing it hard. "Hey!" he cried. "Quit bickerin'. We haven't heard our second choice."

Looking sheepish, Parker and Cassie fell silent.

"Thanks, Jimmy," Captain Jed said softly. Then he sat down on the wagon tongue, seesaw fashion, and continued speaking. "Choice number two is to tar the bottom of your wagon, take off the wheels, and float it across."

"Like a boat?" Jimmy said excitedly.

"Pretty much," replied Captain Jed. "Only you pole it across."

Parker's mind was clicking away. "Floating would save us the fare plus the traveling time to the ferry. And we've already got plenty of tar on hand."

"Sounds like an awful lot of work," Cassie said skeptically.

"No denying that," Captain Jed said.

"But what if we miss some spots and the wagon's not watertight?" Parker asked.

"That's always a risk," Captain Jed conceded. "But if you've a mind to float, I'll teach you how to do it." Captain Jed paused, noticing a look of uncertainty on Parker's face. "Just don't forget," he said, "I promised your pa I'd look out for you. I'd never let you cross in a leaky wagon."

"Would *you* pole us across?" Jimmy asked.

Captain Jed sighed. "I wish I could, Jimmy. But I'm responsible for the entire wagon train. I've got to make sure everyone makes it over okay. But I'll be in the water riding Liberty and working the guide ropes so nobody runs afoul of the current. Besides, it's faster and safer that way."

"If you're gonna be riding your horse, then who's going to be poling our wagon across?" asked Parker.

"Why—*you*, of course."

"*M-me?*" Parker stammered. "I've never even rowed a boat."

Captain Jed rose to his feet. "Son, every step you take on this trail is gonna force you to do something you've never done."

"B-but—" Parker protested.

"No buts," Captain Jed replied. "Whether you ferry or float, I'm counting on you to get this wagon over to the other side." He tipped his hat as if departing. "Now you folks better decide quick what you want to do. There's a nasty storm heading our way. If we don't make it across the Caw tomorrow, we could be stranded here for days."

Cassie stared at Captain Jed in amazement. "How can you be so sure a storm's coming?" she asked. "There's not a cloud in the sky."

"Old Indian wisdom," he said, smiling. "The Caw's rising too fast for April. That means heavy rains upriver. Besides," he added, "I can smell a change in the air. Ain't sure what it means yet. But it smells to me like danger."

FERRY OR FLOAT?

Help the Montgomerys decide whether to take a ferry or "caulk and float" their wagon across the Caw River. Make a chart like the one shown below, then check off which of the statements are true and which are false. Based on your chart, predict what the Montgomerys will do.

	True	False
1. Ferries sink most of the time.		
2. The Montgomerys don't have enough tar to caulk and float.		
3. Caulking and floating would save money.		
4. The wagon might sink if the tarring isn't done right.		
5. Ferry fares are expensive.		

THE LIFELINE

After Captain Jed left to discuss the next day's crossing with other members of the traveling party, the Montgomerys debated their options for a while before finally agreeing that they would float their wagon across the Caw. Captain Jed hadn't meant to scare them with his frank talk—of that the children were sure. The captain, as usual, was just calling things as he saw them. But in light of what he'd said about the high fare and about the chances of bad weather, Parker and Jimmy had both argued strongly against taking the ferry. Parker was especially anxious about entrusting his wagon to a strange ferryman. If a storm was brewing, Parker didn't want to stray very far from Captain Jed's watchful eye.

What swung Cassie over to their side, though, was not the superiority of her brothers' reasoning, but the fact that other people on the wagon train whose opinions she respected were also choosing to caulk and float. The most influential of these people, in Cassie's view, was Ellen McBride, one of the pioneer wives with whom she'd been developing a warm friendship. "Ellen," as Mrs. McBride had urged Cassie to call her, had taken Cassie under her wing and was teaching her to cook so that her two brothers would no longer make gruesome faces at her meals.

As it happened, the McBrides' wagon was parked just two spots down from the Montgomerys', and Ellen had stopped by to offer the children some doughnuts and crabapple jelly she'd made. Finding them going around in circles about the crossing, she'd informed them that she knew of at least five parties—her family, the Hubbards, the Smiths, the Hutchersons, and the loner Rupert Lansing—that were all planning on caulking.

"Indeed," Ellen said in her Irish accent, "there'll be many rivers ahead with no ferries to raft us over. Some, I'm told, are too deep to ford. So before long we'll all be caulking and floating. And if you ask me," she'd added, gently placing the basket of goodies in Cassie's hands, "I'd say it's better to caulk sooner rather than later, because tarring gets easier each time you do it, and the thicker the tar, the safer your wagon."

Cassie had reflected on Mrs. McBride's counsel and been persuaded by her logic. If caulking *was* unavoidable and if several coats provided the best protection, then they might as well get the first nasty coat over with. So with a sigh, she'd taken a bite out of one of Ellen's flavorful doughnuts, murmured a contented "Mmmmm," and announced to her brothers that she'd changed her mind. "Haul out the tar bucket," she'd declared.

During the nooning time—the short lunch break that pioneers allowed themselves—Cassie stole a few precious moments to write an entry in the family trail journal. She was keeping the diary to present to her father as an official record of the family's adventures on the way to Oregon. After she finished writing, she turned the diary over to Jimmy, who illustrated the passage with a skillful sketch of the twisty Caw.

Parker, unfortunately, didn't get a chance to relax or eat anything. He spent his nooning with Captain Jed, going over details of how to make the Montgomery farm wagon as leakproof as a tortoise shell.

Then came the hardest part. For the remainder of the day, until waning sunlight forced them to quit, the three children worked tirelessly alongside Captain Jed to waterproof their wagon. First they unloaded all the food, clothing, blankets, tents, pots and pans, tools, spare parts, and keepsakes that had been crammed into every possible inch of wagon space. Then, with the wagon bed exposed, Parker, Jimmy, and Captain Jed coated the underbelly and inside floorboards and sideboards with a thick layer of tar. For good measure, they pasted a carpet of animal hides down on the inside boards to form another watertight seal.

That night the three exhausted children slept soundly in their bedrolls under the open stars. Neither the distant, hungry howls of prowling coyotes nor the forlorn whistles of fearful quails stirred them from their slumber.

At sunup Captain Jed blew reveille on an old brass bugle, setting off a torrent of groans among the animals and good-natured outcries among the pioneers. A sleepy-eyed Cassie awoke and changed mechanically into her daily work outfit, a calico dress protected by a long white apron. Parker and Jimmy slithered out of their bedrolls soon thereafter and painstakingly revived the previous night's campfire with a handful of leaves, a few cottonwood branches, and much huffing and puffing. Following one of Ellen's recipes, Cassie prepared a hearty breakfast of bacon and flapjacks topped with dollops of Ellen's delicious crabapple jelly.

"I can't believe you made these," Parker said, hungrily gobbling down his flapjacks. "They're almost good."

"And you're almost a gentleman," Cassie retorted.

"More, please," Jimmy said, thrusting out his tin plate.

"See! Someone in our family has manners," Cassie said, throwing Parker a barbed look. Then she loaded up Jimmy's plate with far more food than he could possibly eat.

After breakfast, Captain Jed sat down with the Montgomerys to explain the plans for the crossing. "The Caw's only six hundred feet wide here," he said. "The current's tolerable 'cause the river slows down as it rounds the bend. There will be seven wagons floatin', including the Hubbards' two." He looked into Parker's eyes. "You'll be crossin' next to last, son."

"Why?" Parker asked, unsure whether to feel honored or hurt.

"Insurance," Captain Jed said. "It'll give you time to watch how others do it."

"Who's in front of us?" Parker asked.

"The Smiths—with their daughter Jenny."

Parker started. "You mean, Jenny'll be watching me?"

"They'll probably be busy unloadin' on the other side by the time you cross."

Parker looked relieved. "Who's behind us?"

"Rupert Lansing. He's the fella who joined us west of Blue Mound. He's drivin' two teams of mules. Mules are fast, but they're pesky critters and they panic easy. So I put him last. That way his animals can swim across without feelin' rushed."

"You'll be with us, too—right?" Jimmy said.

Captain Jed shifted his gaze to Jimmy. "Son, me and Liberty and Joe McBride and his horse are gonna be swimmin' right next to you, holding you steady with ropes. We'll be pullin', while you'll be poling."

"Do you still think it's going to storm, Captain Jed?" Cassie asked.

The trail guide looked up and scanned the western skies. A stiff wind was blowing off the prairie, and a row of puffy gray clouds had gathered on the horizon. The rest of the sky was cornflower blue and clear, punctuated only by a red-tailed hawk, gliding high on the air currents, its keen eyes missing nothing that was happening on the ground. As Captain Jed took all this in, Cassie sensed a change in his mood. His lips tightened and he became very still. Abruptly, he sprang to his feet, sounded two loud blasts on his bugle, and shouted, "Crossing time, folks! Everyone down to the Caw— pass the word!" Within minutes, the cry had been taken up and circulated around the wagon train. Soon whips were cracking and oxen were groaning as the parties that had chosen to take the ferry began rumbling out of camp.

Cassie doused the campfire with water. Then she collected all the pots and pans and plates and returned them to a box in the rear of the wagon. After securing the lid, she rubbed her hands clean in the folds of her apron. She threw Parker a meaningful look. "Did you notice?" she said. "Captain Jed didn't answer my question about the storm."

By mid-afternoon all the parties that had voted to float, except for the Montgomerys and Rupert Lansing, had crossed the Caw without incident. Captain Jed and Joe McBride must have shuttled back and forth between the banks on their horses a dozen times. First they would shepherd a family's draft animals across, then they would return to escort the family's wagon.

Parker could feel his stomach knotting up as he watched Captain Jed and Joe McBride deposit the Montgomerys' draft animals on the far shore and head back his way. He knew it would soon be his turn to attempt the passage.

The Montgomery and Lansing wagons lay parallel to one another on the river bank. With their wheels removed to keep them from bogging down on sand bars, they looked like beached whales. Rupert Lansing's mules, still loosely tethered to the wagon yokes, were lapping at the water, waiting to be untied and swum across the Caw.

Upon reaching the river bank Captain Jed dismounted and double-checked the caulking on the Montgomery wagon. He gazed at the sky, which had been growing increasingly dark over the course of the day's crossings. Quickening his motions, he fastened the ends of two long ropes to iron rings on the wagon's underbelly. He passed one free end to Joe McBride, who was sitting atop a chestnut mare, and kept the other himself. Then he remounted Liberty. At Captain Jed's nod, the two men lashed their ropes around the horns of their saddles.

"Ready, Admiral?" Captain Jed called out to Parker.

"Aye! Aye!" Parker responded nervously, planting the end of his crossing pole in the water.

"Ready, Cassie and Jimmy?"

"Ready!" Cassie and Jimmy replied together, waving their poles out the back of the wagon's bonnet.

"Okay, Parker, push off!" Captain Jed yelled. He tugged on Liberty's reins, heading the stallion out into the water. "Hee-yah!" shouted Joe McBride, spurring his mare into the current. The guide ropes grew taut, and with a shudder and a creak the wagon slipped into the Caw.

Parker glanced anxiously inside the wagon. No water was seeping in. "We did it! We're floating!" he exclaimed. Two muffled shrieks of joy erupted from the back of the bonnet.

A third of the way across the river, Parker felt a sharp chill. The wind picked up, and the slate-gray sky suddenly cracked with bolts of lightning. Deafening thunder rolled down the river like an avalanche of stones. The rains came, transforming the smooth surface of the Caw into a sea of choppy goose bumps.

"Captain Jed!" Parker cried out in panic.

"Don't worry!" yelled Captain Jed. "We've got you in tow. It's going to be okay."

Just then Cassie noticed an unexpected problem. Frightened by the thunder and the downpour, Rupert Lansing's mules had stampeded headlong into the river, dragging Rupert Lansing's wagon— and its terrified occupant—after them. The crazed mules were braying loudly and churning up muddy foam. Cassie feared that Rupert Lansing's wagon might capsize. Lacking guide ropes to steady it, the wagon was being buffeted by the current. It tipped dangerously to one side.

"Parker, stop poling!" Cassie screamed. "Tell Captain Jed—Mr. Lansing's in trouble."

Parker glanced back over his shoulder and saw the unfolding disaster. There was no room to crawl back through the wagon, which had been reloaded with family belongings. So without thinking, Parker found a handhold on a rib on the bonnet, swung his body onto the sideboard, and began working his way back to the rear. His heart was pounding mightily.

"Parker! What are you doing!" cried Captain Jed.

Parker pointed to the runaway wagon.

"Dang fool mules!" exclaimed Captain Jed, instantly realizing what had happened.

Another bolt of lightning split the heavens, triggering another explosion of thunder. The rains came even harder now. The current surged.

"The mules are coming straight at us, but they're tiring," Captain Jed called out to Parker. "Throw Lansing a rope—maybe we can bring 'em into line."

"I'll try!" Parker yelled back as he disappeared into the rear of the wagon.

"Do we have anything that floats?" Parker asked Cassie.

Cassie gazed frantically about. She grabbed an empty milk can and pressed down hard on the lid. "Will this do?"

"Perfect. Jimmy—hand me some rope."

Jimmy tossed Parker a coil of rope. Lansing's mules, their energies flagging, were now almost within throwing distance. Parker tied a knot around the can handle and heaved the can into the swirling water. As he'd hoped, it rose to the surface and drifted out into the current.

Rupert Lansing was kneeling on his wagon's seat, struggling vainly to reach the mules' submerged hitching ropes with his crossing pole.

Parker cupped his hands to his mouth. "Grab our line, Mr. Lansing!" he shouted. Lansing looked up and spotted the floating milk can. He leaned forward as far as he dared, and, swinging his pole to the left, snagged the rescue line.

Through the sheets of rain, Parker could see a relieved look on the older man's face.

"Good work, Parker!" Captain Jed cried. "Now fix your end to the wagon, and Joe and I will pull y'all in."

The downpour continued through the rest of the crossing. But Captain Jed and Mr. McBride, on their powerful horses, managed to tow the two wagons in. When the Montgomerys finally reached shore, members of the other pioneer families gathered round in their soaking clothes and cheered. Cassie

and Parker's quick thinking had probably saved Rupert Lansing's life.

Later that evening, after the ferrying and floating parties were reunited at a new base camp, Captain Jed took the children aside.

"You all done me—and your pa—proud today," he said.

The three Montgomerys beamed. Right now, they couldn't imagine a higher compliment.

What's in a Name?

Kansas is home to thousands of species of plants, birds, and other animals. Below are two species mentioned in the story. Use what you know to match them to their correct descriptions, which appear under their scientific Latin names.

1. Red-Tailed Hawk
2. Big Bluestem Prairie Grass

Descriptions:

A. *Ophisaurus attenuatus*: pointed snout, narrow head, long cylindrical body with no limbs; 18-24 inches long; tan, gray, or brown tail breaks off when attacked.

B. *Callipepla squamata*: 10-11 inches long; white-tipped crest, light blue-gray plumage; lives in grassland; nervous and flighty.

C. *Buteo jamaicensis*: 19-24 inches long, light to deep brown plumage, rust-tipped tail; powerful claws; dines mostly on small rodents; keen eyesight.

D. *Helianthus annuus*: 12–24 inches long; gold, red-brown, or yellow; popular landing platform for Monarch butterflies.

E. *Gerardi*: blades up to 12 inches long and ½-inch wide in summer; important food for bison and draft animals.

GHOST WAGONS

The next day dawned sunny and mild, but the effects of the nightlong storm lingered. Mud was everywhere. The pioneers had eaten breakfast in the mud. They had mud on their shoes, mud on their clothes, mud in their bedding and tents, and mud in their hair.

High winds had worked their mischief as well. During the night the bonnet on the Hutchersons' wagon had blown off and become entangled in the undercarriage of the Walkers'. The Hutchersons were sure the bonnet could be repaired, but they reported that three sacks of flour, rice, and cornmeal had been ruined. Two family tents had also been flattened, soaking their slumbering occupants to the bone.

After breakfast, Captain Jed met with members of the wagon train's governing council to discuss the storm damage and the pioneers' marching goals for the day. The council was composed of the heads of household of each traveling party. It had been formed not long after the Missouri crossing to set the rules the pioneers would live by during their six months on the trail.

Pioneer women didn't usually attend council meetings, but Captain Jed had asked Cassie to come along and take notes. He knew, from hearing her read aloud from her journal, that she wrote clearly and accurately. As a trail guide he'd learned that nothing sharpened council members' memories better—or settled disputes quicker—than a detailed record of what people actually said at meetings. But there was another reason he wanted Cassie to serve as the council's unofficial secretary. Having been born into slavery and gained his freedom at the age of twenty-three, Captain Jed had never received a formal education, and so he could neither read nor write. With Cassie as the minutes-taker, he could always ask her to read the record back to him in private without suffering embarrassment.

At the council meeting, Captain Jed raised the issue of the Hutchersons' losses. He also said he was hoping to get the wagons back on the trail soon after nooning. A few council members volunteered to help fix the Hutchersons' damaged bonnet and others agreed to lend the family sufficient provisions to tide them over until the caravan reached St. Mary's Mission, the next trading post on the trail.

"I don't see why us that has should give to them that don't," objected Giles Walker, a burly Pennsylvanian with an unattractive habit of sucking on his lips through missing teeth.

"Well, Giles," Captain Jed replied. "We'll remember those words of wisdom the next time your cornmeal is molderin' in the barrel."

The remark produced chuckles among all the council members except for Giles Walker.

Cassie scribbled furiously.

Then Zebulon Clark, a farmer from Vermont who was traveling with his brother Simon, stood up. He pointed the stem of his clay pipe at Captain Jed and said, "Cap'n, what's the big rush to push on in all this mud?"

"Fair question, Zeb," Captain Jed replied. "Sloggin' through the mud is no particular pleasure of mine, either. But losin' an hour here, a day there, all adds up after a while. Believe me, you don't want to be caught on the east side of the mountains when the winter snows start comin'."

"So you're telling us—?"

"I'm not *tellin'*, Zeb, I'm *proposin'* we strike camp as soon as the Hutchersons' wagon gets fixed."

"I'm with the Captain on this," said Abe Smith, one of the most respected members of the governing council. "Our family's running low on beans and dried fruit. We can spare some rice and flour for the Hutchersons, but we'll be spread mighty thin 'til St. Mary's."

"Vote?" suggested Joe McBride. The other council members nodded in agreement.

Cassie turned over a new page, pencil poised.

Abe Smith cleared his throat. "I move we forget about the mud and hit the trail as soon as possible— just like the Captain said. All agreed say 'Aye.'"

"Aye!" came a loud chorus. Glancing around, Cassie quickly noted the names of the "aye"—sayers.

"Opposed?" Abe Smith intoned.

"Nay!" called out Giles Walker and Frank Johnson.

"'Ayes have it, motion passed," Abe Smith said.

After the meeting broke up, Cassie walked with Captain Jed back toward the Montgomery wagon, trying carefully to sidestep the wheel ruts where muddy water had collected. Even so, the hem of her calico dress became soaked and discolored, causing Cassie to make a disgusted face.

"Seriously, Captain Jed," Cassie said, "how are we going to get our wagons started in all this mud?"

Captain Jed extended a hand to help her over a puddle. "The answer is we're not going to let the mud bog us down."

"I don't follow."

"You'll see. Here's what you do. First go round up your brothers and gather a couple of bushels of grass—the taller the better. When it's time to move out, we'll lay a bed of grass in front of the wheels for traction. With the oxen pullin' and us pushin' from behind, we'll do just fine."

"Will we keep doing this all the way to St. Mary's?" Cassie asked.

"Only if we have to," Captain Jed replied.

Cassie found Parker replacing a broken drawstring on the wagon bonnet. Jimmy was playing nearby with the McBride's dog Luke, a floppy-eared mutt that had taken a special liking to him. Cassie stored the minutes of the council meeting in the family trunk for safekeeping. Then she recounted to her brothers everything that had happened at the meeting and informed them of the grass-gathering chore Captain Jed had assigned them.

"I know where we can get real tall grass," Jimmy said.

Parker and Cassie followed Jimmy halfway around the wagon circle toward a field on a slight rise. The path took them right by Rupert Lansing's wagon. As they approached, a reedy voice called out from inside the bonnet, "I've got wooden toys, you know!"

The three children halted. "Pardon?" replied Cassie. "Was someone addressing us?"

The wagon rocked a little. Pots and pans clanged. Then Rupert Lansing's head poked outside. "Wooden toys—would you like to see 'em?"

"Well, um—" Cassie hesitated.

"Stay right there." Rupert Lansing's head snapped back into the wagon. The wagon wobbled again amid a commotion of rummaging noises.

"What's going on in there?" whispered Parker.

Rupert Lansing wriggled out of the bonnet onto the driver's seat, dragging a large wooden trunk behind him. "Well, don't just stand there," he said to Parker. "Help me down with this."

"Er—okay," Parker said.

Moments later the Montgomerys were all staring at the most beautifully made trunk they'd ever seen. Big as a treasure chest, it had finely etched silver handles, hinges, and locks, and six wooden panels into which intricate imaginary animals had been carved. Jimmy knelt down and ran his fingertips slowly over the amazing artwork. Cassie noticed for the first time that the sideboards of Rupert Lansing's wagon were also decorated with small animal carvings.

"Did you make these animals?" Jimmy asked.

Rupert Lansing nodded.

"And the trunk and the silverwork?"

"Yep." Rupert Lansing groaned as he stretched his back. "When I was younger, I could do almost anything with my hands."

Cassie studied the man closely. He was a tall figure, of thin build, with curly ash-colored hair, gray

eyes, and a long horsy face. He wore wire-rimmed spectacles that magnified his eyes almost to the size of silver dollars. His palms were thickly calloused and his arms nicked and scarred.

Rupert Lansing motioned Jimmy to lean away from the trunk. Then he threw open the lid.

Jimmy's eyes widened. Inside the chest were wooden soldiers, bullroarers, climbing bears, string puppets, whimmydiddles, mountain bolos, hand puppets, hand-carved animals, spinning tops, miniature coaches and carriages, and more.

"Did you make these, too?" Jimmy asked.

"Yep. For my son. He's grown up now. Lives in Oregon. Got kids of his own." Rupert Lansing looked at Jimmy and then at Cassie and Parker. He made a stiff gesture toward the trunk. "So, um... there they are—toys. Help yourself—all of you."

"We really couldn't," said Cassie. "They're for your grandchildren."

Rupert Lansing folded and unfolded his hands nervously. "No, please. You three saved my life. I wanted to thank you properly. There's more than enough for my grandchildren. Please, pick. It would make me happy."

"Okay," said Cassie, sensing it would be impolite now to refuse. She picked a hardwood horse with a silk tassel mane and tail. Jimmy chose a hand puppet. Parker selected a perfect scale model of a clipper ship inserted inside a bottle.

"I reckon I've kept you way too long," Rupert Lansing said after Parker had helped him put the trunk back into the wagon. "You best be going about your chores." He fussed with the arrangement of his spectacles on his nose. "Maybe if you have some spare time," he added, "you can come by and see me at the next campin' grounds?"

"Sure," said Jimmy, "and maybe you could teach me how you made all those things."

"It's a deal, pardner," Rupert Lansing said with a grin.

The Montgomerys were strangely silent as they gathered grass in the nearby field. They didn't quite know what to make of their new acquaintance. Most of the pioneers considered Rupert Lansing unfriendly because he liked to keep to himself and rarely participated in any of the camp's evening activities. After his rescue at the Caw, he'd been so overwhelmed that he'd quickly fled the scene after blurting out a few clumsy words of thanks. But the Montgomerys had just discovered that Rupert Lansing wasn't unfriendly at all. He was just a little lonely and tongue-tied. It was puzzling to them how often—and how badly— grownups seemed to misjudge each other.

As Cassie, Parker, and Jimmy were returning to camp, they spotted a wagon train heading slowly toward them along the muddy trail.

"Aren't they going in the wrong direction?" asked Cassie. "They're moving east."

Parker glanced up at the position of the sun in the sky. "You're right, sis. Let's go see what their story is."

The children put down their bundles and hastened toward the approaching wagons. The lead wagon stopped. An exhausted man left his oxen and limped over to the children.

"We've got sick and hungry people here," he said. "Can I speak with your leader?"

"Sure," said Parker. "Let me show you the way."

"Say, Mister," Jimmy broke in, "are you going to Oregon, just like us?"

"We were, sonny," the man said. "But we turned back. And I hope the good Lord grants you the wisdom to do the same—before it's too late!"

Captain Jed was one of many scouts who helped explore and map the Oregon Trail. Based on what you've read and the information on the map in the front of this book, find the geographical features and locations that are described below.

1. This famous section of the Oregon Trail cuts through a low point in the Rocky Mountains.

2. This fort is located in the Cascade Mountain range.

3. The Oregon Trail crosses this river about 150 miles west of Fort Kearney.

4. The Montgomery family started at this jumping-off point.

5. Independence Rock is east of which mountain range?

CHAPTER 4

"You!!"

Daniel Everett, the head of the ill-starred wagon train that had just lumbered into camp, sat on one of Captain Jed's buffalo robes in front of the Montgomery campfire, sipping a cup of coffee. His face was wind-burnt and his eyes looked dull.

Several members of his traveling party were huddled around the fire too, draped in borrowed blankets. Captain Jed and the leaders of the governing council sat opposite Everett, while Cassie and Jimmy looked on from the wagon, and Parker and his friend, Jon Hubbard, straddled the wagon tongue. Everyone was waiting to hear why the Everett party had reversed its course.

"We were twelve wagons out of Independence about two months ago," Daniel Everett began. "Now we're just seven. Our guide, Luther Killibrew—"

Captain Jed started. "*Killibrew!* That no good—!"

"You know him?" Daniel Everett asked.

Captain Jed nodded. "All too well. He's slipperier than an eel. He had no business takin' anybody west so early. The prairie grass ain't hardly grown for animals to feed."

"So we found out," Everett said.

"Go on," Joe McBride said.

Daniel Everett took a long swig of coffee. "After we ran through our animal feed, our oxen couldn't find good grazing, so they got weaker and weaker. Then a few drank bad water and died. That left us with too few animals to pull our wagons, so we had to start tossin' belongings out onto the trail to lighten the loads."

"Whereabouts were you?" asked Seth Hutcherson.

"Just shy of the Platte River crossing."

"That's a mighty tricky river," Captain Jed commented. "How'd the crossin' go?"

"All right, at first. The river weren't deep. So Killibrew told us we should lead our animals across. But straight off, several mules got sucked down by quicksand and drowned.

Cassie gasped in horror. "Oh, how awful!" she whispered to Jimmy.

Daniel Everett went on. "So we had to dump even more baggage by the wayside and squish a bunch more families into single wagons. That's when we all started grumbling about how Luther Killibrew weren't worth a cent we paid him."

Captain Jed tossed a branch into the fire, watching the coals erupt in red flares. "Where's Luther now?" he asked. "Back in one of your wagons?"

"No," Daniel Everett replied. "He done absquatulated."

"You say he *took off*?" exclaimed Seth Hutcherson.

"Yessir, with a strongbox full of cash that our families had set aside for dealin' with disasters."

"Any idea where he might be?" Captain Jed asked.

"None at all. We tried pushin' down the trail ourselves for a while. But we didn't have a guide, and we were short on money, animals, and supplies. So we figured it was best to quit and turn around while most of us was still alive."

"You lost folks?"

"Four," Daniel Everett said grimly.

Captain Jed shook his head sadly. "Maybe we can help," he said. "But we're tryin' to make St. Mary's Mission in a few days. We've got to break camp this afternoon. Why don't you folks stay here and rest up? There's fresh water, decent huntin' in the fields, even scrub for firewood. We're short on provisions ourselves, but I'm sure we can spare some grub for you and some feed for your animals."

"That's uncommon kind of you, Captain," Daniel Everett said. "There's just one more favor I'd like to ask," he said, rising from the robe. "We've got a sick man with a ragin' fever. He cut his leg bad. Now the infection's streakin' up his thigh. He needs attention quick."

Captain Jed didn't hesitate. "We can take him with us. There's a man here who once worked in an army field hospital. If he can keep the infection under control 'til St. Mary's, there's a good chance your man'll pull through."

"I'm deeply grateful, Captain," Daniel Everett said.

"No thanks necessary," Captain Jed replied. "Just carry your man—"

"Caleb Shrike."

"Just carry Caleb Shrike over to Rupert Lansing's wagon. Anyone here can direct you to it."

As Daniel Everett and the members of his party returned to their wagons, Captain Jed signaled to Parker to ready the draft animals for departure. Then he sent Cassie and Jimmy to alert Rupert Lansing that the sick man was heading his way.

Rupert Lansing's face lit up when he saw Cassie and Jimmy. But his expression turned grave when they informed him of the purpose of their visit. "I was in the army during the Seminole Indian Wars," he said. "I helped doctors treat plenty of infections. I hope I can help now." Turning to Jimmy, he said, "Son, climb into my wagon. Fetch me the black box and the green book on top of the fold-down table."

Jimmy scampered into the bonnet, curious to see the inside of Rupert Lansing's wagon. The interior was neatly, even lovingly, arranged. It had perfectly carpentered cubbies and shelves, boxes with hinged lids, and a set of stackable chests that somehow fit snugly into the curvature of the bonnet. Pots and pans dangled from hooks on the wooden bows.

Nailed to the side of one cubby was a set of engravings of scenes from an Indian village. All these drawings bore the name of the artist—"Rupert Lansing"—at the bottom. Jimmy quickly located the fold-down table, grabbed the book and black box, and exited the rear of the bonnet to the ground.

Rupert Lansing lifted the lid on the box and checked its contents—bandages, needles, thread, scissors, a razor, and several small stoppered bottles with powders, twigs, and leaves in them. "I've everything I need," he said. Then he turned to Cassie and handed her the book.

"What's this?" she asked.

"You like to read?" he asked.

"Very much."

"I've had this book—*Riddle Me This*—since I was a child. I'd like you to have it. It's full of jokes and puzzles."

This time Cassie didn't protest. She loved books practically more than anything, and she'd only been allowed to pack three of hers to take on the journey—*Pilgrim's Progress*, *McGuffey's Reader*, and *The Pathfinder*.

"Thank you, Mr. Lansing," she said.

"You're welcome, child," Rupert Lansing said. "Now all we have to do is wait for our patient."

Soon two men appeared carrying a board with the injured man stretched out on it. "Where do you want him?" one of the bearers asked.

"Right here," Rupert Lansing said. "I need to clean his wound. I'll put him in my wagon before we get under way."

The men lowered the board to the ground. The sick man was lying on his back, moaning, with one arm slung over his eyes. His right pant leg had been cut off, revealing a wrap of bloody rags around his calf. Rupert Lansing knelt down beside the injured figure. He lifted the man's arm to feel his forehead for fever.

Rupert Lansing gasped as he caught sight of the man's face.

"What's the matter, Mr. Lansing?" Cassie asked.

At that moment, the half-delirious man opened his eyes. From somewhere inside him came an angry growl. He pointed a bony finger at Rupert Lansing and cried, "You!!"

Then he lost consciousness.

The book that Rupert Lansing gave Cassie contained the following riddles. Can you guess the answers?

1. What is in seasons, seconds, centuries, and minutes but not in decades, years, or days?

2. Why is a baker a foolish person?

3. What increases the more it is shared?

CHAPTER 5

SONGFEST

It was Saturday evening. The day's marching was over, and all across the wagon circle small fires blazed in shallow trenches to shield them from the wind. The tender notes of a fiddle, accompanied by the sweet strains of a mouth organ, wafted on the soft night air, and the savory aroma of bacon and beans lingered over the campsite. Parker and Jimmy wandered down to the main campfire to join a group sing, while Cassie sat by the flickering Montgomery campfire, writing in her journal:

Saturday, April 22, 1848

We've had such a stretch of bad weather since we crossed the Caw. I doubt we've made even ten miles! After we set out for St. Mary's on Thursday, it rained for a spell, cleared up, then hailed at night. On Friday afternoon the winds were so fierce we had to stop and chain the wagons together to keep them from blowing over. Parker and Jimmy and I crawled into our wagon and pulled the drawstrings on the bonnet closed. We lay there waiting and waiting for the howling to quit.

I was surprised we could all fit inside. When Mr. Lansing took in that sick person—Caleb Shrike—he had to make room in his wagon. So Parker and I offered to take in a few of Mr. Lansing's things (such as his toy chest) as well as some of Mr. Shrike's belongings. The extra baggage hasn't bothered Jimmy at all. Mr. Lansing told him he could open up the toy chest. By now Jimmy must have examined every single toy!

I'm gradually getting to know Mr. Lansing better because I've been helping him care for Mr. Shrike. I may be wrong, but I think Mr. Lansing and Mr. Shrike have met before and that Mr. Lansing is scared of Mr. Shrike for some reason. Every time Mr. Shrike stirred in his sleep, Mr. Lansing seemed to tremble. And once, when Mr. Shrike was out of his head and babbling nonsense, I heard Mr. Lansing muttering something under his breath. It sounded like "why are you still hounding me?" What could that mean?

Whatever bad feelings that might exist between the two of them, though, Mr. Lansing appears to be giving Mr. Shrike good care. He stitched up Mr. Shrike's wound and stopped the infection from spreading. This afternoon Mr. Shrike's fever broke and he seemed less delirious. Mr. Lansing said he expects his patient to be up and walking soon. But I could tell Mr. Lansing wasn't too happy about

"Cassie, stop writing!" a voice called out. "The singing's half over." It was Jimmy. He'd come charging up to drag his sister back to the songfest.

"Hold your horses!" Cassie said. She carefully closed her journal, tucked it safely away in the wagon, then followed her insistent younger brother toward the source of the music-making.

Seated on blankets around a large campfire were members of most of the traveling parties—the McBrides, Hubbards, Smiths, Clarks, Hutchersons, and Walkers. All eyes and ears were fixed on the entertainers of the night: Abe Smith on fiddle, Simon Clark on banjo, Giles Walker on mouth organ, and the lovely-voiced Ellen McBride and Emily Hutcherson leading the singing.

As the group finished a rendition of *Polly Wally Doodle*, Cassie and Jimmy settled down next to Captain Jed on his buffalo robe. She noticed Parker and his friend Jon sprawled out on a blanket between Captain Jed and Jenny Smith.

"Did Mr. Lansing come?" Cassie whispered to Captain Jed. "I told him to try."

"Ain't seen him, Cassie," Captain Jed replied. "Can't make a man do what ain't in his nature."

Cassie sighed. "I know. I was just hoping."

Abe Smith twisted a tuning peg on his fiddle and sawed his bow back and forth across the strings until he produced a pure tone. He tapped his foot and winked at Simon Clark. On cue the group sprang into a spirited version of *Skip to My Lou*. Soon everyone was singing along, children and adults alike. As the last notes faded, the crowd gave the group a warm ovation. Then Giles Walker declared a brief intermission and Virginia Smith passed a jug of cool water up to the thirsty performers.

Cassie gazed up at the sky, idly wondering if there might be another pioneer girl elsewhere on the trail who was staring up at the same stars as she was. Her musings were disturbed by a heavy thumping noise behind her. She turned to see a man limping toward them with the aid of a cane. Captain Jed turned too.

"Howdy, folks," the new arrival said. He tipped his hat to Cassie, then at Captain Jed, and said, "They tell me you're the trail guide."

"They say right," Captain Jed replied. "Glad to see you're better, Mr. Shrike. You had a mighty bad gash."

"I seen worse," Caleb Shrike allowed.

"Maybe so. But you could've lost that leg. Rupert Lansing pulled you through. You really owe him."

"More than you know," Caleb Shrike said.

"Come join us," Captain Jed said. "Take a seat."

"Thank you kindly, but no," Caleb Shrike responded. "Now that I'm up and around, I'd like to get my things and set up my own tent. You wouldn't happen to know where my gear's at, would you?"

"Sure do," Captain Jed said. "It's in the Montgomery wagon." He turned to Parker. "Son, you want to show Mr. Shrike where his bags are stashed? Then maybe you could help him set up his tent."

Parker rose. "Be glad to. Where should I set him up? Near us?"

Captain Jed shook his head. "It's best he be close to Lansing—just in case that leg acts up again."

"Maybe I should return Mr. Lansing's chest and things too," Parker suggested. "I'll be going that way anyway."

"You can't carry all those things by yourself," Captain Jed observed.

Jon Hubbard jumped up. "I'll help."

"All right," Captain Jed said. "But make it quick. We've got some hard marches ahead and I don't want to see you two losing too much sleep."

"We won't," Parker said. He motioned to Caleb Shrike. "Follow us. Our wagon's not far." Then the two boys, accompanied by the limping Caleb Shrike, slowly headed off toward the Montgomery wagon.

Cassie gave a shiver. What did Caleb Shrike mean when he said he owed Mr. Lansing "more than you know."

Music was an important part of pioneer life. Here are some lines from songs the pioneers sang and you've probably sung as well. See if you can select the correct titles of these tunes from the list below:

1. "My country, 'tis of thee,
    Sweet land of liberty,
    Of thee I sing." (1831)

2. "[Song Title] how sweet the sound,
    That saved a wretch like me,
    I once was lost but now am found,
    Was blind but now I see." (Published in 1835)

3. "Be it ever so humble there's no place like home!" (1823)

4. "[Song Title], won't you come out tonight
    And dance by the light of the moon." (1844)

Song Titles

A. "Buffalo Gals"

B. "Polly Wally Doodle"

C. "Home on the Range"

D. "America the Beautiful"

E. "O Susanna"

F. "Home Sweet Home"

G. "Suzy, Dear Suzy"

H. "Amazing Grace"

I. "America"

CHAPTER 6

"QUICKSILVER"

The significance of Caleb Shrike's remark became clear the next morning. It was Sunday and the pioneers had just concluded a brief prayer service before preparing to hit the trail again. Two of Walt Hubbard's oxen had slipped through the wagon circle during the night, and Parker had teamed up with Zeb Clark and Walt Hubbard's two oldest sons, Jon and Matt, to round them up. In Parker's absence, Cassie and Jimmy packed up the wagon and watered the animals. Then they went to ask Captain Jed about the proposed departure time of the wagons.

Cassie and Jimmy found Captain Jed among a group of pioneers clustered beside Rupert Lansing's wagon. Cassie saw immediately that something was wrong. Rupert Lansing was propped on the board above the jockey box with his hands and feet bound and a gag across his mouth. Sitting on a wagon hub with a rifle in hand was Caleb Shrike. At his feet were Rupert Lansing's toy chest and a slim wooden case.

"What's going on?" Cassie whispered to Captain Jed. "Why's Mr. Lansing tied up?"

"Shh! child," Captain Jed said.

Ellen McBride was wagging a finger furiously at Caleb Shrike. "I don't care if you have proof you're the Queen of Arabia," she was saying, "this man"— she pointed to Rupert Lansing—"nursed you back to health. And *this* is how you repay him? For shame!"

"I'm no minister, ma'am, I'm a bounty hunter," Caleb Shrike replied coolly. "I've been tracking this man for over a year. Now I've caught him."

The crowd buzzed when it heard the words "bounty hunter."

Rupert Lansing squirmed more violently in his seat.

"Untie him, Shrike!" Joe McBride demanded.

"Criminals belong in jail; they don't deserve special treatment," Caleb Shrike retorted. "This man is wanted in five states for counterfeiting, and I aim to claim the $500 reward for bringing him in."

Abe Smith stepped forward. "Let's all just simmer down, " he said, addressing the entire crowd. Then he shifted his attention to Caleb Shrike. "We're law-abiding people here. Nobody's going to interfere with justice. But if I'm not mistaken, our Constitution says a man is innocent until proven guilty. We may be miles from civilization, but it's still our policy."

"As it should be," Caleb Shrike said obligingly.

"Good," Abe Smith replied. "Then you won't mind putting down that rifle and untying Mr. Lansing. If you've got evidence he committed some crime, I'm sure the governing council won't stand in your way."

The bounty hunter rested his rifle against a wagon wheel. "My proof is in there," he said, gesturing toward Rupert Lansing's toy chest and case. "So before I release my prisoner, I'd like to hand these over to the council for safekeeping."

"Agreed," remarked Abe Smith.

The instant his bonds were removed, Rupert Lansing leaped off his wagon and lunged at Caleb Shrike, angrily declaring his innocence. Captain Jed and Abe Smith had to forcibly separate the two men to prevent an ugly fight. At Captain Jed's suggestion, Abe Smith had the two men escorted to "neutral" wagons at opposite points in the camp.

"Mr. Lansing is no criminal, I just know it," Cassie said to Captain Jed later as she and Jimmy accompanied him on his wagon rounds.

"Look, child," Captain Jed replied. "You might think he's a good man and I might too. But we know nothin' about his past. He could be hidin' something."

"So could Caleb Shrike," countered Cassie.

"Yep, him too."

Shortly after nooning, Abe Smith called an emergency meeting of the governing council. Cassie was once more called upon to take notes. She was seated on a long bench next to Abe Smith and the accused, Rupert Lansing. Parker and Jimmy, not wanting to miss a word, had curled up on the grass beside her. Captain Jed stood nearby, ready to react if Rupert Lansing couldn't control his rage again.

"Present your evidence," Abe Smith said to Caleb Shrike.

The bounty hunter approached the bench slowly, the tip of his cane making deep impressions in the soft earth. He handed the chairman a large discolored sheet of paper.

"What's this?" Abe Smith asked.

"A 'wanted' poster, issued by the U.S. Marshall's Office in 1847."

Abe Smith examined it. "Why, I don't see Lansing's name anywhere on it."

"You won't," replied Caleb Shrike. "The poster describes a master forger known only by his nickname—'Quicksilver.'"

"Is this a picture of Quicksilver?" Abe Smith asked, squinting at a water-stained drawing.

"Yes. But only one lawman before me ever got a look at him. That's why the sketch is so bad."

The councilman gazed at the picture and then at Rupert Lansing. "I'm sorry, Mr. Shrike," he said. "I'm not sure I see a close resemblance." He passed the poster down to the other council members. Most said they weren't sure whether it was Lansing or not. The bounty hunter snatched back the poster and directed the council's attention to Quicksilver's description underneath the picture. "It says, 'white male, southerner, 5'11", 160 pounds, late forties, curly hair, light-colored eyes.' Fits Lansing perfect. We first crossed paths in St. Louis. That's how I learned that his real name was Rupert Lansing. I thought I had him then, but he gave me the slip."

"Liar!" Rupert Lansing roared. "You know we met ten years ago—in the army!"

"Quiet, Rupert!" Abe Smith cautioned. "Your turn will come." He gave the bounty hunter a long stare. "So far, Mr. Shrike, I haven't seen anything that links Mr. Lansing to any crime. What other evidence do you have?"

The bounty hunter asked Giles Walker to retrieve Rupert Lansing's toy chest and wooden case. Then he had him dump their contents out on the grass before the councilmen.

"Stop!" cried Rupert Lansing. "There's nothing in there but toys!"

"No more outbursts, Rupert!" Abe Smith directed.

Caleb Shrike picked through the pile of toys. Suddenly something gleamed in the sunlight. The bounty hunter fished out two highly polished rectangular metal plates and handed them over to the council. They had fine lacey lines etched into their surfaces. "I found these hidden in Rupert Lansing's toy chest last night. They're engraver's plates for printing counterfeit bills. There's only one man who could make plates of this quality—the master counterfeiter known as Quicksilver."

"I never saw those plates before in my life!" Rupert Lansing screamed.

"Silence!" Abe Smith ordered.

The councilmen appeared shaken by the revelation. After a long silence, Walt Hubbard asked, "What's in the other case, Mr. Shrike?"

Caleb Shrike lifted the lid. Inside the case were engraving tools, several blank plates, and scores of neatly bundled bills.

"Every one of these bills is counterfeit," the bounty hunter said. "It all begins to add up, doesn't it? Quicksilver is a master craftsman, so is Rupert Lansing. Quicksilver makes almost flawless engravings, so does Rupert Lansing. The engraving tools I showed you are Rupert Lansing's. Rupert Lansing had Quicksilver's plates and bills hidden inside his wagon. Rupert Lansing fits the description of Quicksilver on the wanted poster." He paused to let all of this sink in. "What more evidence do you need?" he concluded. "Rupert Lansing may seem like just some some regular feller, but he's none other than Quicksilver, the notorious counterfeiter."

"Are you finished?" Abe Smith inquired.

"Yes," the bounty hunter replied.

"Thank you, Mr. Shrike," Abe Smith said. Then he turned to Rupert Lansing and said, "Rupert, you've heard Mr. Shrike's charges. How do you answer them?"

Rupert Lansing rose, shaking with rage. "Caleb Shrike is a liar!"

"Are these your engraving tools, Rupert?" Seth Hutcherson asked.

"Yes, but I use them to make plates for printing drawings, not money."

"How do you account for the counterfeit plates and bills then?" questioned Abe Smith.

"Shrike must have planted them."

"For what reason?"

"Revenge. You see, we served together in the army. I reported him for stealing army property and he went to prison. He swore if he ever saw me again, he'd get even. I don't know where he got all those bogus plates and bills, but I'm innocent. If anyone's a criminal, it's him!"

"I never served in the army with Rupert Lansing!" Caleb Shrike shot back. "That man will say anything to avoid arrest."

The three Montgomery children jumped to their feet. "Mr. Lansing's telling the truth about the toy chest," Parker exclaimed. "It was stored in our wagon for a couple days. There was nothing in it but toys."

"And I played with them all," said Jimmy.

"'Fraid that isn't much in the way of proof," Seth Hutcherson commented. "Mr. Lansing could have hidden the plates elsewhere in his wagon and then returned them to the trunk last night."

"It's just not fair to judge Mr. Lansing so quickly," Cassie objected. "Last night he was a free man, today he's facing jail. If he says he's being framed, I believe him, and I think we owe it to him to investigate."

Abe Smith shook his head. "I know you three have good intentions," he said. "But this is no business for children. Mr. Lansing is facing very serious charges, and we can't let our feelings influence our decisions."

SPEAK "PIONEER"

People in the 1800s used many words that seem strange to us today. Here are a few of these words. Three definitions appear under each. Only one is correct; see if you can guess which one.

1. **Catarrh (ke-TAR)**

   A. Native American word for antelope.

B. An inflamed nose and throat.

C. A horn for storing gunpowder.

2. **Felloe (FELL-oh)**

   A. Rim of a multispoked wagon wheel.

   B. Another word for a friend.

   C. A mosquito bite.

3. **Leeverites (LEE-vur-ites)**

   A. Items pioneers had to dump or "leave" behind on the Oregon Trail.

   B. Iron bolts that locked a wagon's brake lever.

   C. The first name for blue jeans.

4. **Miasma (mee-AZ-ma)**

   A. A swamp gas thought to cause disease.

   B. A type of square dance.

   C. A steep mountain pass.

5. **Saleratus (sal-ur-RAT-tis)**

   A. A gum disease pioneers got.

   B. The period between "lights out" and dawn.

   C. Another word for baking soda.

CHAPTER 7

EVIDENCE!

Abe Smith ordered that Rupert Lansing and Caleb Shrike be returned to their "neutral" wagons so that the council could deliberate in secret session. In the debates, the council found itself deadlocked over the issue of Rupert Lansing's guilt or innocence. It was also divided over the question of whether the wagon train should depart as planned for St. Mary's with Rupert Lansing's fate undecided. Many of the pioneers had taken to heart Captain Jed's frequent reminders that a wagon train that is not moving forward is losing ground. But another group, led by the McBrides, agreed with the Montgomery children that it was wrong to hand Rupert Lansing over to the bounty hunter without a closer examination of Rupert Lansing's charges that he was being framed.

The McBride group said it believed Parker and Jimmy when they'd said they were familiar with every item in Rupert Lansing's toy chest. The members of the group also wondered why a counterfeiter would want to hide illegal plates in a toy chest that he'd encouraged children to come and explore.

Those who seemed to be siding with Caleb Shrike argued that the bounty hunter had had too little time to plant the plates and bills among Mr. Lansing's things. And in any event where did Mr. Shrike get such evidence in the first place?

The two groups were evenly divided. So when Parker and Cassie proposed a last-ditch plan to prove Rupert Lansing's innocence, a majority of council members, weary from debate, were ready to listen.

"We don't know anything about Caleb Shrike and his motives—except for what Mr. Lansing says," Cassie explained. "But if we let Parker ride back to the Everett encampment, maybe he can find out who Mr. Shrike is and why he was heading west with them."

Giles Walker, the head of the anti-Lansing group, shook his head. "It's a waste of time. He'll probably find nuthing'."

"It's a risk, I grant you," Cassie replied. "But I know in my bones that Caleb Shrike is lying—only, I don't know why he's doing it or how he got hold of those plates and bills. Maybe somebody in the Everett party can answer those questions."

"I agree with Cassie," said Joe McBride. "We're all good folk here. How many of us would rest easy knowing we sent the wrong man to jail?"

"How much time do you need, Parker?" Abe Smith asked.

"A day, at most."

"You fixin' on riding alone?" asked Frank Johnson.

"I was hoping to take Jon with me—as a witness."

"That okay with you, Walt?" Abe Smith asked.

Walt Hubbard nodded. "My son knows how to take care of himself."

The council chairman turned to Captain Jed. "Can we spare the day, Captain?"

Captain Jed thought for a moment. "I reckon we can make up the time if we add some extra walking time to the days after."

With Captain Jed's support firmly behind it, the Montgomery plan passed the council. "We'll meet again tomorrow when Parker and Jon return," Abe Smith declared. "We'll see then if they have any news to report."

Jon borrowed one of his dad's horses, while Captain Jed lent Parker Liberty to ride. "He's smart," Captain Jed said, patting Liberty on the flank, "and won't give you no trouble."

Parker and Jon rode faster than they had ever ridden before. By evening, they arrived in their former base camp west of the Caw crossing. They were relieved to find the Everett party still there and its pioneers much rested and refreshed following their horrible ordeal.

Daniel Everett was surprised to see them. Venison was cooking over the campfires, and the leader of the party invited Parker and Jon to share in their evening meal. He was happy to hear that Caleb Shrike had recovered. But when the two boys explained to him the purpose of their visit, Daniel Everett blanched. He immediately summoned the two men who had been the board bearers for Caleb Shrike, and a third man who had shared a wagon with Caleb Shrike during their journey west.

Over dinner Parker and Jon listened to the men's stories in stunned silence. Afterwards, Daniel Everett spoke up. "If you'd like, I'll ride back with you tomorrow to testify about what was said here

tonight. It's the least I can do. You good folks showed us uncommon kindness, and I'd like to repay it."

Parker and Jon nodded and thanked the mild-mannered man. Then they hauled out their sleeping gear and grabbed some much-needed shut-eye, resting content that their quest had not been in vain, and that tomorrow they would be able to answer most of the important unresolved questions about Caleb Shrike and Rupert Lansing.

The governing council reconvened in the early afternoon, following Parker and Jon's return, accompanied by Daniel Everett on his horse. Caleb Shrike had not been informed of Parker and Jon's mission, and he did not witness their arrival with Daniel Everett. This all fitted well in Parker and Cassie's strategy.

At the meeting, the bounty hunter sat on a boulder to the left of the council members puffing on a pipe. Rupert Lansing, once again, was seated on a bench beside Cassie and Abe Smith, while Parker, Jimmy, and Captain Jed stood nearby.

"Before we hear from those speakin' for Rupert Lansing," Abe Smith said, "I think we should let Caleb Shrike say his piece."

Caleb Shrike got up from the rock with the aid of a cane and turned to face the council. "You've already seen the evidence. The plates. The bills. The tools. It proves that Rupert Lansing is a thief and a liar." He paused to wipe his brow. "He's passed his bad money in the east, and now he's heading west to pass his bad money there. Don't let him make fools of you. Turn him over to me so I can bring him to justice." He stopped and made an awkward bow. "That's all I have to say."

"Thank you, Mr. Shrike," Abe Smith said. He pinched the bridge of his nose and turned to Rupert Lansing. "Rupert, do you have anything to say?"

"Y-yes, sir, I do," Rupert Lansing said.

At that moment, Parker stepped forward. "If you don't mind, Mr. Smith," he said, "Cassie and I would like to say a few words first. "

"I object!" protested Caleb Shrike. "The kids have nothing new to offer. They're just wasting our time."

"But we *do* have new evidence to offer, Mr. Smith," Parker replied.

Caleb Shrike looked startled. "That's impossi—

"I'm allowing Cassie and Parker to testify, Mr. Shrike," the chairman said. "That okay with you, Rupert?"

Rupert Lansing nodded silently.

"I object!" Caleb Shrike screamed again.

"Overruled," Abe Smith said. He turned to Cassie. "Perhaps you'd like to go first?"

"Thank you, Mr. Smith," Cassie said. She put aside her pencil and pad, straightened the folds in her skirt, and rose to address the assembled group. "When I started on this wagon train," she said, "I didn't know any of you here. But slowly I got to know many of you. Ellen here"—she pointed to her friend—"is one. She's got family of her own to care for, yet she's been looking out for me and my kin. And with her help, I believe I've been doing a better job looking after my kin." She turned to face Captain Jed. "Captain Jed here is my pa's best friend, and he's getting to be one of ours too. He's like our compass. We'd truly be lost without him.

"All of you were once strangers to me until something happened that made you not strangers anymore. That's the way it is when people get to know other people. And that's what happened to me and my brothers with Rupert Lansing. The fact that he might be standoffish or clumsy with words doesn't mean he isn't a good man."

Caleb Shrike coughed loudly. Cassie threw him a sharp look.

"Now some of you may say that someone young like me can't judge the worth of people," she continued. "Well, I respectfully beg to differ. Going down this trail makes you grow up fast and helps you get to know who's your friend and who's not. I'm going to leave talking about the facts of this case to folks who know the facts. But I will say this—we should all be proud to have Rupert Lansing traveling with us. He is no outlaw, and I have nothing but contempt for a man like Caleb Shrike who would wrongly accuse another man for personal gain."

"Who's wrongly accusing who?" Caleb Shrike snarled, shaking his cane at her. "My work is dangerous, and I get paid to keep criminals from—"

"That's enough, Mr. Shrike," Abe Smith interrupted. "Parker, are you and Jon ready?"

"Are you gonna listen to some wet-behind-ears kids?" the bounty hunter fumed.

"Ought to," Parker replied, "especially when they hear what we found out." Parker faced the council members. "First off," he began, "me and my brother Jimmy feel the same about Rupert Lansing as my sister said. Everyone knows, though, that that wouldn't be enough to save him if he was guilty. But the honest truth is that he isn't. Mr. Shrike here is trying to pull a hoax on all of us, a hoax so evil I can't understand it."

"This is no hoax, sonny," Caleb Shrike replied.

"Let's see 'bout that," Parker said. He motioned to Jon, who went around the back of the Johnsons' wagon, which was parked nearby, and returned with their guest, Daniel Everett.

Caleb Shrike's face turned ashen. "What is this?" he cried.

"Do you still want to stick to your story?" Parker asked.

"I object to that fella being here!" Caleb Shrike bellowed. "He knows nothin' about this case."

"He knows plenty," Parker said. "The most important thing he knows is that Rupert Lansing is not 'Quicksilver.'"

"How do you know?" Frank Johnson asked Daniel Everett.

"Because the man called 'Quicksilver' was on our wagon train. Mr. Shrike tracked him down and arrested him just before we reached the Platte River."

"Lies! All lies!" Caleb Shrike shouted.

"We were all shocked," Daniel Everett continued. "We didn't know who the man really was. But Mr. Shrike found dozens of plates and a fortune in phony bills in Quicksilver's wagon. Caught the man red-handed and then the fella up and confessed."

"So Caleb Shrike actually had 'Quicksilver' in custody?" Joe McBride said.

"Yes," Daniel Everett said.

"But where is he now?" Abe Smith asked.

"At the bottom of the Platte," said Daniel Everett. "He was one of the four who drowned—never had a chance with those handcuffs on."

Parker picked up the story from there. "So when the Everett party turned back and met us, and Caleb Shrike saw Rupert Lansing, he figured he could pin the crime on him. Mr. Lansing fit the description. The law wasn't sure exactly what 'Quicksilver' looked like, and besides, he knew Mr. Lansing from ten years ago, and had a grudge against him."

"So Shrike was hoping to pocket the money and get rid of an old enemy at the same time," Abe Smith observed.

"That's right," Parker replied.

"What do you have to say for yourself, Shrike?" Joe McBride asked.

"I tracked Quicksilver for near to a year," Shrike snarled. He turned to Parker "And I'd have my reward money if not for you and your meddling sister."

"I helped too," called out Jimmy, swinging his legs freely on the bench.

"Frank, Simon, Seth, Zeb—take our Mr. Shrike back to his tent and see he stays there," Abe Smith said. "We'll make sure he's turned over to the authorities when we get to St. Mary's."

The four men whose names had been called out quickly surrounded the spluttering Caleb Shrike and herded him away. Abe Smith then turned to Rupert Lansing and said, "It's over, Rupert. You have nothing to fear now. You still want to say something?"

Rupert Lansing looked at the crowd of assembled pioneers. He rubbed his hands together nervously. "I'm not a person as gifted with words as Cassie. I mostly talk with my hands. That is, I *work* with my hands and let my *work* do the talking for me. I'm no thief. I'm not a crank. I'm just a person. I never meant to cause a fuss. I just wanted to go quietly out to Oregon to settle near my brother." He looked anxiously from Cassie and Parker and Jimmy to the others. "I guess I've been rescued twice by these good children. Maybe if we can all be friends, that'll count as a third rescue." He looked down. "That's all."

Tears welled in Cassie's and Ellen McBride's eyes. Parker went up to Rupert Lansing and slapped him on the back. Then Jimmy appeared at Rupert Lansing's side and tugged at his arm.

"When you going to show me how to draw and carve wood like you," he said.

"Soon, Jimmy, soon," Rupert Lansing replied.

Captain Jed smiled. "Listen up, folks," he said. "We can still make some distance before nightfall. Let's get ready to move out!"

"I SENTENCE YOU TO...."

There were no police or courts to enforce the law on the Oregon Trail, so groups like the governing council had to do it themselves. Sometimes the punishments inflicted were severe.

One wagon train sentenced a thief to be tied to the ground in the hot sun for hours. Another group banished a murderer from its wagon train, forcing him to leave his wife and children. If you had the power to decide Caleb Shrike's punishment, what would it be? Why? Do you think a person like Caleb Shrike could ever change?

Words to Know

bonnet (BON-it): curved cloth top of a covered wagon.

bullroarer: a flat piece of wood attached to a string that a child twirls around to make a "roaring" sound.

caulk and float: process of sealing a wagon bed to enable it to float across a river.

cholera (KAHL-er-a): serious, contagious disease of the small intestine.

corral (KER-ral): a fixed enclosure or a wagon circle for protecting livestock.

draft animals: animals such as oxen or mules used to pull heavy loads.

emigrant (EM-i-grant): person who leaves one region or country to live in another.

ford: to cross a river by walking, by riding an animal, or in a vehicle.

hoax (HOXE): an act intended to deceive or trick people.

mountain bolo (BOE-low): a toy made up of two small balls joined by a string. The object of the game is to jiggle the string is to make the two balls rotate in opposite directions.

nooning (NOON-ing): lunch break for pioneers.

pioneer (pie-o-NEER): settler in a new or unknown area.

quicksand (QWIK-sand): bed of loose sand and water that can suck down creatures that walk on it.

scow (SCAU): flat-bottomed boat with squared-off ends.

venison (VEN-i-son): deer meat.

whimmydiddle (WIMMY-dih-dle): a toy composed of a "rubbing" stick and a notched stick with a pinwheel at one end. When the first stick it is rubbed along the second, the pinwheel turns.

yoke: crossbar with two u-shaped pieces that encircle the necks of draft animals pulling a load.

How Did You Do?

Check your answers below.

Chapter 1
1-F, 2-F, 3-T, 4-T, 5-T

Chapter 2
1-C, 2-E

Chapter 3
1. South Pass
2. Ft. Vancouver
3. The S. Platte River
4. Independence
5. The Rocky Mountains

Chapter 4
1. *There are no "ns" in decades, years, or days.*
2. *Because he sells what he kneads (needs) most.*
3. *Happiness.*

Chapter 5
1-I, 2-H, 3-F, 4-A

Chapter 6
1-B, 2-A, 3-A, 4-A, 5-C

Chapter 7
One that might have occurred to you is that this was not the first time Caleb Shrike did something wrong. On the other hand, Caleb Shrike did seem to be good at his job. He managed to recover the counterfeiting plates and phony bills from the real Quicksilver, even if he didn't succeed in bringing Quicksilver back for trial. It's interesting, as well, to wonder what Caleb Shrike might have done had he not chanced upon Rupert Lansing. Do you think he would have returned the plates and bills to the government? Was it worth it to stage such a hoax?

About the Author

Award-winning author Mel Friedman has written dozens
of books for children and teenagers. Mel lives in New
York City and is the co-author of Ride to Rescue, an
Oregon Trail Adventure, and the author of The Mystery of
the Backlot Banshee, a ClueFinders Mystery Adventure.

Check out these other

OREGON TRAIL® ADVENTURE

Novels!

WESTWARD BOUND!

The Montgomery children first set out from Independence, Missouri for Oregon to reunite with their father. The children must rise to the challenges of life on the trail while coping with the recent loss of their mother. When Jimmy is lost in a dust storm, his older siblings grow to trust their frontier guide, Captain Jed, to find him, and understand the resourcefulness they will need on their journey.

COMING SOON!

RIDE TO RESCUE

A sudden deadly illness grips the Montgomery wagon train. Only Parker has the strength to ride to the nearest fort and to get the medicine they need. Parker encounters many challenges and dangers as he journeys alone on horseback to Fort Childs. He comes across Pawnee Indians, who don't quite fit the dangerous description he's been led to believe.

Available wherever books are sold or online at www.learningcompanybooks.com.